D0633530

This book belongs to:

_____

KLASKY CSUPO INC. Based on the TV series *Rugrats*® created by Arlene Klasky, Gabor Csupo, and Paul Germain as seen on Nickelodeon®

SIMON SPOTLIGHT
An imprint of Simon & Schuster Children's Publishing Division
1230 Avenue of the Americas, New York, New York 10020

Tommy Catches a Cold copyright © 1998 Viacom International Inc. All rights reserved.
Thank You, Angelica; Oh, Brother!; Reptar's Surprise Visit; Twin Trouble; and *Chuckie Visits the Eye Doctor* copyright © 1999 Viacom International Inc. All rights reserved.
Open Wide! copyright © 2000 Viacom International Inc. All rights reserved.

NICKELODEON, *Rugrats*, and all related titles, logos, and characters are trademarks of Viacom International Inc.

All rights reserved including the right of reproduction in whole or in part in any form.
SIMON SPOTLIGHT and colophon are registered trademarks of Simon & Schuster.

Manufactured in the United States of America
10 9 8 7 6 5 4   ISBN 0-689-84166-3

These titles were previously published individually by Simon Spotlight.

NICKELODEON®

Rugrats™

Bestest Stories Ever!

Simon Spotlight/Nickelodeon

New York   London   Toronto   Sydney   Singapore

Contents

Chuckie visits the Eye Doctor

by Luke David

illustrated by Barry Goldberg

One morning a long time ago, Tommy and Chuckie were playing Reptar. "Rrrrr! Rrrrr!" growled Tommy. He held his Reptar at arm's length and shook him fiercely.

Chuckie held his Reptar close to his face and squinted. "Rrrrr-rrrrr?" he said.

Next Tommy and Chuckie played tag. Chuckie was it. "Got you!" said Chuckie as he reached to tag an armchair. *Wumpf!* Chuckie bumped into the footstool. "I thought the chair was you, Tommy!" laughed Chuckie. He picked himself up.

"You're still it, Chuckie," said Tommy, giggling. "Try to get me."

Then Chuckie tried to tag the TV. *Clonk!* Chuckie tripped and fell. "Ouch!" said Chuckie. "I got a boo-boo on my head. I don't think I like this game, Tommy."

"Okay," said Tommy. "Let's do something else."

Just then Stu walked in. "*Dummi Bears* is on, boys." *Zap!* He turned on the TV. Tommy and Chuckie sat together on the floor to watch.

"I can't see," said Chuckie. He scooted forward. "I still can't see too well," he said. He scooted forward again. "That's better." Chuckie was sitting smack in front of the screen.

"Whoa now, buddy," said Stu. "You're too close." He picked Chuckie up and moved him back. Chuckie started to cry.

"Aw, don't cry, Chuckie," pleaded Stu. "Y'know what? It's too nice a day to be cooped up in here. Let's go outside and play in the backyard."

Chuckie could hear his dad and Tommy's mom talking.

"It's awfully nice of you to help me aerate the lawn, Chas," said Didi.

"My pleasure," replied Chas. Then he saw the babies coming. "Hey, Chuckie, come to Dad!"

Chuckie toddled across the grass toward Chas.

Chuckie toddled right into a small tree. *Thud!* He was knocked flat on his behind.

"Oops!" said Chuckie.

Chas picked Chuckie up and hugged him. "Poor little guy! Funny, but that used to happen to me all the time before I got my glasses. . . ."

"Chas?" Didi asked gently. "Do you think maybe it's time for Chuckie to get his own pair of glasses?"

"He was sitting smack in front of the TV, as if he couldn't see," added Stu.

Chas nodded. "Y'know, I was just about Chuckie's age when I got my first pair of glasses. I'll call right away for an appointment at the eye doctor."

19

"TOMMY!" said Chuckie. "The regular doctor is bad enough. Just think how scary an eye doctor must be!"

"It might not be so bad, Chuckie," said Tommy. "Remember how I didn't want to get my rooster shot, but then in the end it didn't hurt at all, and the doctor gave me a lollipop?"

"Maybe your rooster shot didn't hurt, but mine scared the poop out of me!" said Chuckie.

"The eye doctor can squeeze us in this afternoon, Chuckie," said Chas. "Don't worry, son. Wearing glasses isn't so bad. Lots of people do. I do and so does Tommy's Grandpa."

"Conflabbit!" said Grandpa Lou. "I feel like a human windshield wiper. Why, it took me *fifteen* years to get used to wearing glasses."

"Don't mind him, Chuckie," said Chas. "It's fun to wear glasses. They help you see everything better. Didi, is it okay if Tommy comes with us to make Chuckie more comfortable?"

"Of course," said Didi. "It will be educational for Tommy."

"Nice to meet you, Chuckie," said Dr. Pedop. "You can sit here, right between your dad and your friend."

"See!" whispered Tommy. "She looks nice."

"First let's test your dad's eyes," Dr. Pedop beamed a tiny flashlight right into one of Chas's eyes, then into the other. Chas smiled.

"Okay, Chuckie," continued the doctor, "you and Tommy can try the lights on each other." Tommy and Chuckie zapped the lights on each other's face. They giggled.

"Now I'll try it on you, Chuckie," said the doctor.

"It doesn't hurt at all, Tommy," whispered Chuckie.

25

"Now, Chas, you read the chart," said Dr. Pedop. "I'll point to one of these big E's and you use your finger to show me which way it's pointing."

"Now it's your turn, Chuckie."

"Okay, see this cool machine? It's like a pair of binoculars, but instead of looking at something far away, we use it to look at eyes up close," explained Dr. Pedop. "You try it on your friend, Chuckie, and then I'll try it on you."

27

"You did really well, Chuckie!" said the doctor. "The good news is that you're going to get an extra pair of eyes. They're called glasses, and lots of people wear them. Now, would you and your friend like lollipops?"

"Chuckie, I'm so proud of you! You were a brave boy during that eye exam," said Chas. "And, Tommy, thanks so much for helping Chuckie."

"And now for the fun part, Chuckie," said his dad. "You get to pick out your own frames!"

"You know what, Tommy?" said Chuckie. "It wasn't that bad after all. Glasses make everything look better!"

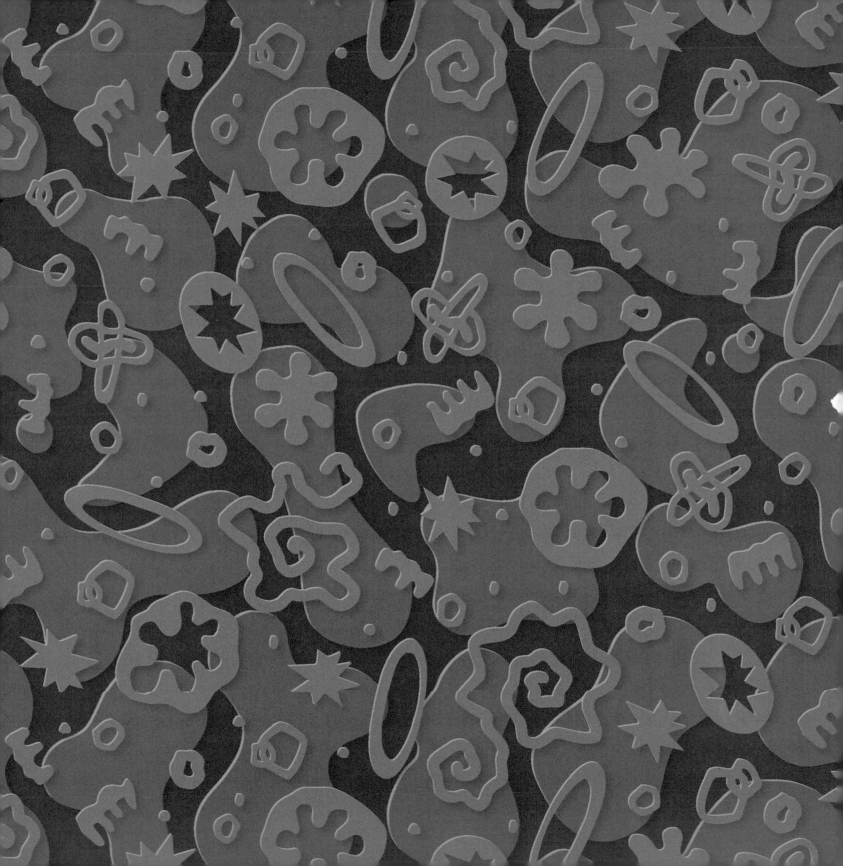

Thank You, Angelica

The Rugrats
Book of Manners

by Cecile Schoberle
illustrated by Ed Resto

"Time for an afternoon snack," announced Didi Pickles, Tommy's mom. Tommy and his friend Chuckie were playing in the den.

"Oh, boy!" said Tommy. "Maybe it's Yummy Fruitso juice."

Didi brought in a tray with cups of fruit juice. "Angelica, would you please bring those cookies from the kitchen table?" she asked. Angelica, Tommy's cousin, carried in a big plate of fresh oatmeal cookies. "Of course, Aunt Didi," she replied in her sweetest voice.

Didi said, "Thank you, Angelica," and went back to the kitchen to bake some more cookies.

"I get to carry the plate of cookies because *I'm* grown up," said Angelica. "I know lots more than you babies do."

Chuckie looked over at the TV. On it, a queen in a fancy crown was smiling at people. "Why are those people bending their heads down?" asked Chuckie. "Did they lose something?"

"No! They have good manners," said Angelica.

Tommy asked, "What's 'manders'?"

"It's 'manners'!" yelled Angelica. "It means being extra nice."

"Hey, everyone, look how people are throwing flowers at the queen's car. I wonder if she'll throw back some of those colored rocks," said Chuckie.

"Of course not! She's not going to *share* her jewels," said Angelica.

"Mommy tells us to share our toys," said Tommy. "Is that good manders?"

"Manners!" yelled Angelica.

"Angelica," asked Chuckie, "does the queen have bad manners?"

Angelica shook her head. "You babies are driving me crazy!"

"Uh-oh, Angelica is mad," said Phil.

43

"Come on, Chuckie," said Tommy. "Let's share something. You can play with my ball. Can I play with your truck?"

"Vroom, vroom!" said Chuckie. He loaded up his dump truck with oatmeal cookies, and sent it rolling across the table. Faster and faster it raced toward Tommy.

"Uh-oh," said Chuckie. The dump truck screeched.

Wham! A big cookie flew out the back. It knocked the hat off Angelica's doll.

"Cynthia!" Angelica screamed.

Kersplash! The dump truck smacked into the cups, splashing juice all over the place. Spike wagged his tail and licked Angelica's juicy face. Tommy and Chuckie rolled on the floor and laughed.

"You babies have terrible, awful manners!" yelled Angelica.

"Gee, Angelica," said Tommy. "Could you get us good manders?" Angelica frowned. She brushed oatmeal cookie crumbs out of Cynthia's hair. "Well, maybe . . . I will show you how to play 'good manners,'" she said. "But I must be . . . queen! And you babies will serve me." She put on her Burger Doodle crown.

BURGER DOODLE

"Yay!" cheered Tommy. "We're gonna get good manders."

Angelica sat Cynthia in a tall chair. "Queen Angelica and Princess Cynthia would like another cookie, please," she said.

"Peas? But we don't have any peas!" said Chuckie.

"PLEASE!" yelled Angelica. "That word is the first good manner. And don't use that dumb dump truck."

Chuckie carefully gave Angelica a cookie. "Should I say something, Angelica?"

"Not yet! Wait your turn. You do what I say." She took a big bite out of the cookie. "Queen Angelica will now show you the second good manner. Your gracious queen says, 'Thank you.'"

Spike snuck up behind Angelica. He snatched her cookie and ran. "Stop it!" she yelled. "It's bad manners to play with food. Especially mine!"

Tommy leaped up. "I serve the queen. I will save her from the cookie-eating monster!" He started chasing Spike.

"No! No!" said Angelica. "It's *bad* manners to run around the table. Or to talk with your mouth full!"

"I'll get him, Tommy," said Chuckie. He leaned out of his chair and grabbed at Spike.

"Don't! Sit still! Sit up straight in your chair! I am a queen!" screamed Angelica.

Spike thought this was a fun game. He ran to Angelica and woofed in her face.

"Ooo, yuck!" squealed Angelica. "Cover your mouth when you cough."

Tommy and Chuckie lunged for Spike. "Look out!" Angelica yelled and jumped back.

Her beautiful Burger Doodle crown flipped off her head. "I'll get it, Your Majesty," called Tommy. He jumped up as high as he could.

"Awesome!" said Phil and Lil together.

"Let me, Your Highness," called Chuckie.

"Woof!" barked Spike.

"Be good! Act nice! Do what I say!" yelled Queen Angelica.

51

"Whoa!" yelled Tommy and Chuckie as they came down. Zoop! The crown settled down right on . . . Spike's head!

Tommy and Chuckie laughed loudly. "Let's call him King Spike,"
said Tommy.

"You babies have terrible, awful, bad, bad manners!" scolded Angelica. "You spilled juice all over. And smushed the cookies. And knocked off Cynthia's hat. And now . . . you took my Burger Doodle crown!"

"Gee, Angelica. We didn't mean to. Did we, Tommy?"
said Chuckie.

Didi walked into the room. "What a mess!" she said.

Angelica pointed her finger at the babies.

Tommy chuckled and
waved his hands.
Didi giggled. "Are you saying you're
sorry, Tommy?"
Chuckie did the same thing. "Isn't that nice?
Chuckie is sorry too," said Didi.

"Yeah, well, I'm more sorrier!" said Angelica.

Didi gave them all a big hug. "Such good kids! Such good manners!" she said.

Then Didi turned and saw Spike. "Mmm . . . that's funny," said Didi. "How did that crown get on Spike's head?"

Oh, Brother!

by Luke David

illustrated by Louie del Carmen and James Peters

Tommy smiled. He had built a tall block tower all by himself. Tommy was very proud.

Then his baby brother, Dil, swiped the top block away. "Look at Dil grab," exclaimed their mother Didi. "He's mastering fine motor control. It's wonderful."

Dil swiped another block. The tower came tumbling down. Tommy was annoyed.

"I don't remember Tommy using such fine hand-eye motor coordination until he was much older," said Stu, their father.

Didi gave a quick nod. "And see how well Dil can hold up his head."

"Amazing!" agreed Chuckie's dad, Chas.

Tommy looked at Dil. Then he toddled over to Chuckie. "I can hold up my head," whispered Tommy. "And you can too, Chuckie. We big babies are just as good as little ones. At least I think we are. Don't you, Chuckie?"

"Well, I don't know, Tommy. The growed-ups seem to think your baby brother is pretty special," answered Chuckie. "It's Dil, Dil, Dil all the time!"

"But the growed-ups love us, too, Chuckie," replied Tommy. "I'm sure of it!"

Just then Dil put his foot in his mouth.

"Wow!" said Stu. "Now *that's* coordination. Yep, Dil's a chip off the old block."

"Oh, Stu!" said Didi. "Dil is adorable."

"If Dil is a doorbell, I don't see why we can't be doorbells too!" Tommy said as he gave Chuckie some finger cymbals. "Maybe then the growed-ups will think we're great too."

Then Tommy dug some bells out of the music crate for himself. *Ting-a-ling-a-ling! Ding-ding-ding!* They rang the cymbals and the bells all at once.

Didi plugged her ears. "Boys!" she called. "Please stop that racket."

Tommy looked sad. Dil blew a bubble with his drool.

"No doubt about it," said Chas as he coochie-cooed Dil under the chin, "little babies are delightful."

"If Dil is light-full," said Chuckie, "we can be light-full too. C'mon, Tommy!"

"Yowee, Chuckie!" complained his dad. "You're shining that flashlight right in my eyes. Please turn it off."

Now Chuckie was sad too. But Didi didn't notice. She said, "You'll remember, Chas, from when Chuckie was tiny, that caring for an infant is not always easy . . ."

Dil interrupted. He bubbered his lips with his finger. "Bubber-bubber-bubber." Then he smiled at his mom.

71

Didi beamed. She gave Dil a quick kiss. "Still, Dil certainly can be angelic."

"Angelica!" said Tommy. "Now they think Dil is like Angelica! What's so good about her anyway?"

"Nothing," answered Chuckie. "Angelica is mean and she's naughty."

"Eggs-actly, Chuckie!" said Tommy. "But if the growed-ups want more Angelica, that's what we'll give them!"

Didi brought the kids into the living room.

"Okay, Chuckie," whispered Tommy. "If we're going to be like Angelica, we've got to act like Angelica."

"I don't know, Tommy," answered Chuckie.

"Well, I do!" said Tommy. "If Angelica wanted the growed-ups to pay attention to her instead of Dil, she'd just hide the baby. Watch!"

Tommy dropped his blankie on top of Dil's head.

"WAAAAAAAAGH!" Dil wailed.

Dil yanked the blankie off his head. He waved
his fists. He kicked his legs. He opened his mouth
wide and screamed, "WAAAAAAAAGH!"

Didi and Chas dropped what they were doing.
Neither knew how to stop Dil from crying.

"I'll get his Binky," said Chas. He ran upstairs.
"I'll get his bottle," said Didi. She dashed into the kitchen.

"WAAAAAAAAGH!" Dil kept wailing.

"See what you get for being like Angelica, Tommy?" said Chuckie. "What do we do now? How can we get Dil to stop crying?"

"Maybe we should go back to being our regular selves," said Tommy. He smiled at his baby brother. Then Tommy picked up a toy train. "Choo-choo-choo-choo!" He drove it around Dil's cushion. "Choo-choo-choo-choo!"

Chuckie made funny faces. Dil cried a little less.

Tommy played peekaboo with Dil. Dil dried his eyes.
Then he started to giggle.

Didi came back with Dil's bottle and Chas came
back with his Binky. But Dil was already okay.

This time Didi scooped up Tommy. She looked down at Dil. "Well, Dil," she said. "One thing is certain—you're *very* lucky to have a big brother like Tommy."

"And a friend like Chuckie," added Chas, and he gave Chuckie a big hug too.

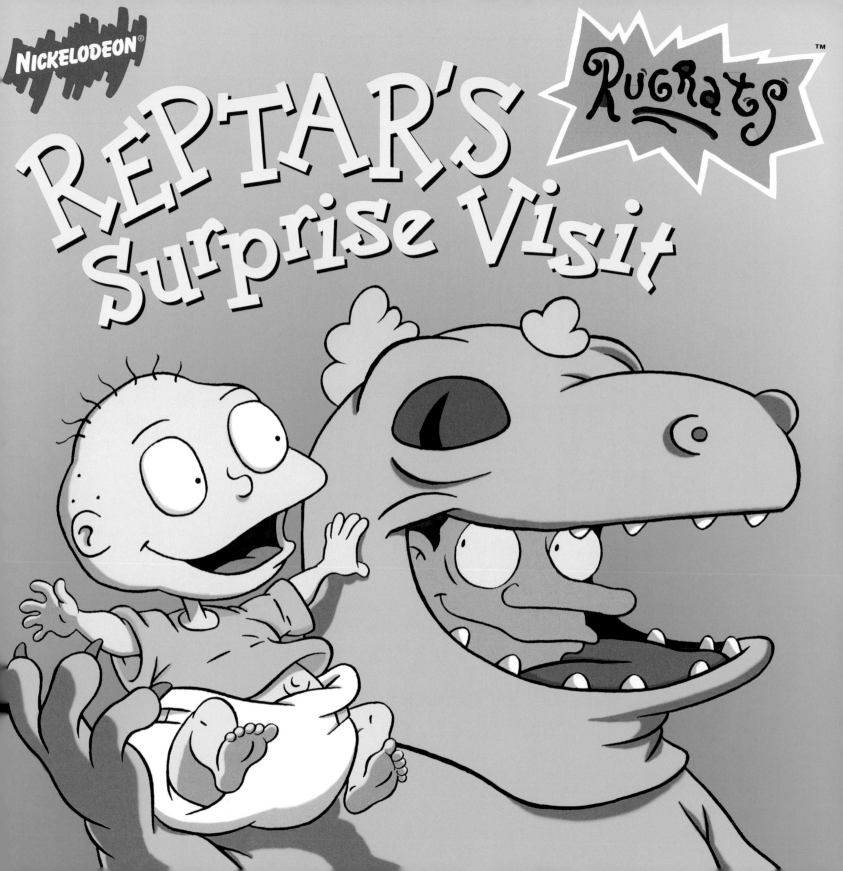

REPTAR'S Surprise Visit

by Cecile Schoberle
illustrated by Steve Haefele

"Tommy, dear, I have some great news!" called his mom, Didi Pickles. Tommy and the babies were playing at his house. "Remember when we were at the mall, and you drew that picture of Reptar? Well, you won a contest, and Reptar's coming to visit this Friday afternoon!" she said.

"Did you hear that?" Tommy exclaimed. "Reptar! My hero! I wonder what it's going to be like having a famous big star here?"

"Do you think Reptar's too big a star to get through the door?" asked Chuckie.

"Nah, Reptar can do anything!" said Tommy. "I can't wait to get a pitcher with me and him to show everybody!"

"Wow! You're going to have a monster at your house, Tommy!" said Phil. He waved his arms and pretended he was a huge creature.

"Reptar's not a monster, Phillip. He's a dinnersaur," said Lil.

"He's *not* coming for *dinner*," said Phil. "He's coming for lunch."

"I hope *we're* not dinner," said Chuckie.

91

"I bet Reptar's going to bring a big cake for us," Tommy said. Suddenly Angelica was all ears. "Is it going to be a chocolate cake?" she asked.

"I hope Reptar's bringing some nice, gooey worm pies," said Phil.
"Yummy!" said Lil.

"I wonder if Reptar will bring Tommy a special surprise?" Chuckie asked.

"What kind of surprise would a dinnersaur bring?" Lil asked.

"If he brings a new Cynthia Sandy Dandy Beach House, you can give it to me," said Angelica.

"I just want my pitcher with Reptar," said Tommy.

Every day that week, Tommy kept thinking about Reptar. He couldn't wait to have his hero come to his house.

At last it was Friday.

Dingdong! The doorbell rang.

"He's here! It's . . . w-w-wow . . ." Tommy started to exclaim.

"So that's your big green hero?" Angelica asked.

"He's big and green, at least," said Susie.

Reptar came in the front door and waved. The babies waved back. All except Angelica. "That Reptar sure doesn't look like the Reptar I saw on TV." Angelica frowned.

Tommy was upset. "Well . . . it does so look like him, Angelica," he whispered back.

"Are you ready to start the games, Mr. Reptar?" asked Stu. All the babies cheered!

reserved for Reptar

Reptar took out a red balloon and a green one and blew them up. Then he twisted the balloons together and handed them to Susie.

"Wow!" said Susie. "It's a pony!"

Pop! A balloon broke in Reptar's hands.

Angelica frowned. "I think Reptar's a phony!"

"No, he's not!" Tommy protested. "Reptar broke that balloon to show how strong he is, just like on TV when he breaks the bad guys' swords and stuff!"

"C'mon, guys! Let's get Reptar something to drink," said Tommy. "And then I'll get my pitcher taken with him!"

"Here's some juice, Reptar," said Tommy. "Oops!"

Splash! The cup went flying, and red, sticky punch dripped down Reptar's face.

"Mmmfff!" said Reptar.

"Was that a Reptar roar?" asked Chuckie.

"Maybe it was a Reptar sneeze?" said Susie.

Didi saw Reptar's red face. "Is it time for face painting already, Mr. Reptar?" she asked.

"Wait a second!" said Angelica as she pointed at Reptar's back. "That can't be the *real* Reptar. He's got a zipper up his back!"

"Maybe it's a boo-boo he got from fighting the Purple Aliums," Tommy said.

"And how come his belly's so big?" Angelica demanded.

"I don't know. Maybe he eats a lot of that yummy Reptar cereal," answered Tommy.

Reptar took more treats out of his bag. He passed around wash-off Reptar tattoos, and plastic Reptar fangs.

"Oh, you children look so scary!" exclaimed Didi, when she saw them. "Those teeth should help you eat this Reptar cake!"

When the babies finished eating their cake, they all joined
hands and stood around Reptar. The babies all circled in one
direction, while Reptar circled in the other.

"Ring around the Reptar, ring around the Reptar," they sang along
with the lady's voice on the tape player. The music got faster. So the
babies went faster. Reptar tried to keep up with the music too.

"Reptar, Reptar, time to fall . . ." the voice sang.

Now everyone was spinning really fast. Reptar was spinning very fast too, until he stepped on a big patch of green icing.

"DOWN!" everybody screamed.

Kaboom! Reptar crashed to the floor, kicking his big green feet in the air.

The babies all laughed. They thought it was part of the game.

Then it was time for a game of Reptar hide-and-seek.
Reptar was "It."

"That phony Reptar won't be able to find anybody!" said
Angelica.

"Sure he will, Angelica," said Tommy. "Reptar's good at
hunting bad guys in the movies. He always finds them."

Stu put the camera on the patio table. "You know, Didi,"
he said, "I loved hide-and-seek when I was a kid. I think I'll
surprise Tommy and play too."

As Stu climbed into the oak tree, he chuckled. "Reptar will
never find me up here."

All of the babies looked for a good
hiding spot. But Tommy had a plan.

Reptar was still dizzy from playing ring around the Reptar. He began to search for the babies anyway.

Tommy couldn't wait any longer. "Now, Susie! Take my pitcher now!" he whispered.

"Okay, Tommy," Susie called out. "Hey, Reptar! Say cheese!"

Tommy gave a big smile as Susie pressed the camera button. The bright flash went off in Reptar's eyes. He blinked wildly.

Just at that moment, Angelica jumped and tried to pull off Reptar's head.

"Okay, big guy, let's see what's under this mask!" she yelled.

"Angelica! Leave Reptar alone!" said Tommy.

Angelica slid off of Reptar's back, and Reptar stumbled toward the tree.

107

Stu climbed farther out on the tree limb to see what was going on.

Craaack! The branch broke! Stu fell toward the ground! Just as Stu was about to crash, Reptar ran underneath the tree.

Kaboom! Stu landed on top of Reptar! They both tumbled to the ground.

"My hero!" Tommy exclaimed.
"Reptar saved my daddy!"
The babies cheered, "Hurray for Reptar!"

It was time for all the babies to open the surprises Reptar had brought them. But Tommy was already holding his most special present of all: his picture with Reptar.

Angelica looked at the photo of Reptar and said, "I still think he's kind of funny-looking!"

But Tommy didn't hear Angelica at all.

"Reptar is the bestest hero in the whole wide world!" he exclaimed. The rest of the babies couldn't agree with Tommy more!

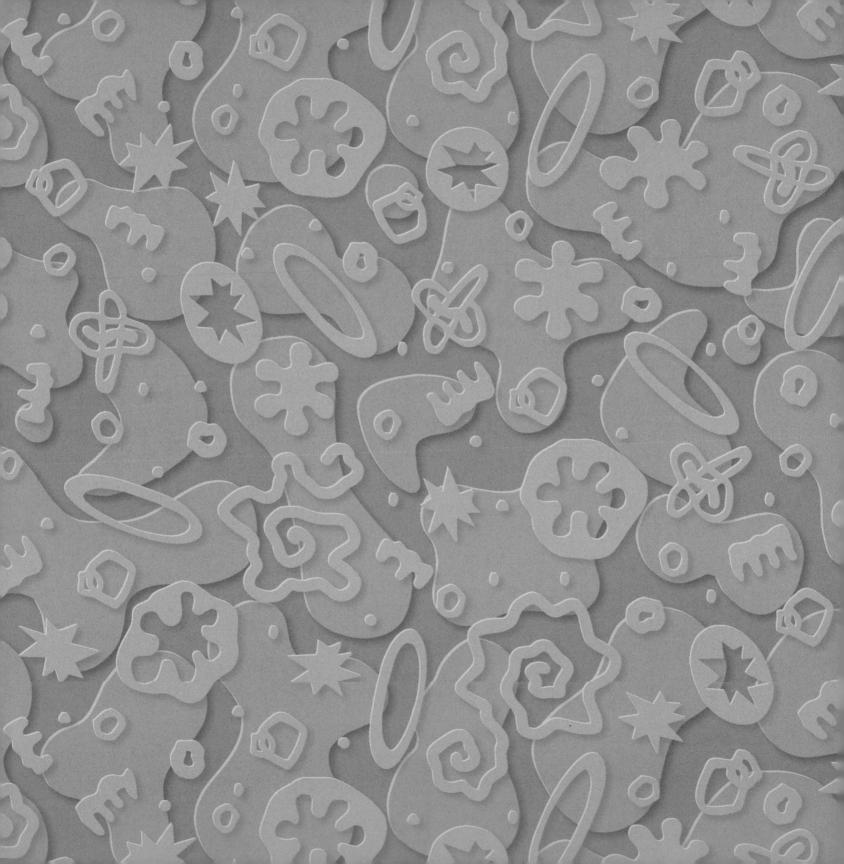

TWIN TROUBLE

by Luke David

illustrated by Barry Goldberg

"Give me that rattle, Phillip!"
yelled Lil. She gritted her teeth.
"No, Lillian. It's MINE!" yelled Phil. He
curled his lip and snarled at his twin sister.

"Is not, Phillip!" said Lil. "The rattle is MINE!" Lil pulled with all her might. Phil pulled with all his might. The rattle went flying to the other side of the room.

"WAAAAAAAAGH!" wailed Lil.

"WAAAAAAAAGH!" wailed Phil.

"Holy smokes!" said Betty, picking up her twins. "I know my pups like to bark, but . . ."

Lil reached across her mom to pinch Phil. Phil reached over to pinch Lil back.

"WAAAAAAAAGH!" both twins screeched at once.

"That's it," said Betty. She dragged Phil away from Lil and gave him to Didi.

"They do seem awfully unhappy," said Didi.
"I heard a Lipschitz audio-sleep-tape on twins
the other night. He suggests treating
twins as individuals for their
greater well being."

"For once that old windbag might have a point," said Betty. "We *have* been acting like the twins are attached at the hip. Maybe that's what's eating them. Come to think of it, Howard dressed Phil in Lil's clothes yesterday and vice versa. We didn't even notice until bathtime."

"Oh, dear," said Didi. "Y'know, Lucy Carmichael dropped a box of hand-me-downs off the other day. Maybe you can find some outfits in there that encourage each twin's individuality."

Betty changed the twins' clothes. "Bingo!" she said.

"Interesting choices, Betty," said Didi. "You're defying gender stereotypes by encouraging imaginative play in Phil and professional aspirations in Lil!"

"Yep," agreed Betty. "These new togs are just the ticket."

"And no more two-for-one toy sales for us!" said Betty. She handed Lil a dump truck and Phil a baby doll. "It's different toys for you two from here on in!"

"Oh, brother!" said Lil to Phil.

121

"And now for the final stage in my game plan: separation!" continued Betty. "Deed, you take Phil upstairs, and Stu will take Lil down to the basement!"

"Well, all right, Betty," answered Didi, "but I'm afraid the twins will miss each—"

Betty checked her watch. "Gotta go. Time for my power swim around the lake. See ya!"

123

"WAAAAAAAAGH!" cried Lil to Chuckie. "I miss Phillip."

"It's all right, Lil," said Chuckie. "Just pretend I'm Phil."

"Okay, Chuckie," said Lil. "You can eat that waterbug if you want. I don't mind."

124

"Lil, yuck, that's disgusting!" said Chuckie.
"Face it, Chuckie," said Lil. "You're not even a teensy
bit like Phillip. I miss my twin brother!"

"WAAAAAAAAGH!" cried Phil to Tommy. "I miss Lillian."

"It's okay, Phil," said Tommy. "Just pretend I'm Lil. Whaddya say we eat these dust bunnies?" Tommy popped a dust bunny into his mouth. "Plegh!" He spit it out.

"No, Tommy," said Phil. "If you want to be like Lillian, you gotta swallow it." Phil popped a dust bunny into his mouth, chewed it, and gulped. "Num-num!"

"WAAAAAAAAGH!" cried Phil to Tommy. "I still miss Lillian."

"Don't worry, Phil," said Tommy. "I have a plan." Tommy picked up his cup-and-string phone. "Come in, Lil! Come in, Chuckie. Over and out!"

"This is ground control, Major Tommy," answered Chuckie.
"We gots to get these twins back together," said Tommy.
"Make a break for it and rendez-moo in the kitchen in oh-five-jillion-seconds."
"Copy," answered Chuckie. "Over and out."

"These stairs are too steep and scary to climb," said Chuckie.
"I gots to get back to Phillip," said Lil. "We gots to figure out a way!"

"Lil, Chuckie," said Stu, "do me a favor and wait here while I run Dil's new and improved Kangaroo up to the kitchen."

"Eureka!" said Lil.

"Drat! My dad's new high-security stair-gate is up!" said Tommy.
"But don't worry, Phil. I have a plan!"

"Funny, this basket seems heavier than usual," said Didi as she lugged the laundry downstairs.

All the babies met in the living room.
"Lillian!" yelled Phil.
"Phillip!" yelled Lil.

"Nothin' seems any fun without you," said Phil.
"Being a twin is a prettyful thing," said Lil.

"We tried to keep them separated," explained Didi, "but they do seem happier together."

"Well, you know what I've always said," said Betty. "When twins are happy, everyone is happy."

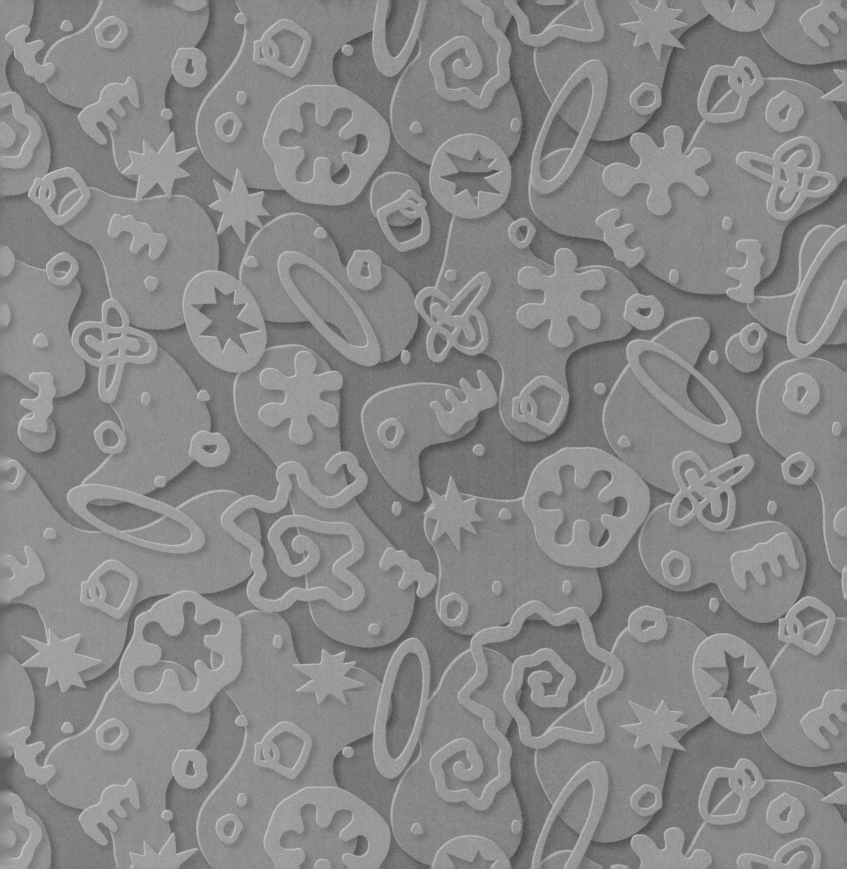

Tommy Catches a Cold

by Sarah Willson

illustrated by Barry Goldberg

On a cold winter day, Tommy and his friends played at the park.

Tommy waddled over to a park bench. He picked up a bottle and took a drink.

Suddenly a shadow fell over him.

"Hey! Thadz *mide*!" said a strange-looking kid with a red nose. Surprised, Tommy handed it to him.

"Hmmm," said Tommy's mother, Didi. "Dr. Lipschitz says that fresh air is good for kids, even in winter. But it looks like there are lots of children here with colds."

"Yep," agreed Betty. "Let's get the kids home before they catch one."

The next morning Tommy woke up feeling strange. His nose didn't work right. His throat tickled.

When Didi saw Tommy she panicked.

"Stu!" she called to Tommy's father. "Tommy is sick!"

"Call an ambulance!" cried Stu, rushing into Tommy's room.

"Ah, pshaw!" said Tommy's grandpa. "The little sprout just caught a bug is all."

"A bug?" Tommy muttered to himself.

"I'll call Dr. Lipschitz," said Didi.

"But it's 5:30 on a Sunday morning!" said Grandpa Lou.

Didi was already racing to the phone. She spoke for a long time, and wrote down a lot of instructions.

Later that morning Stu took Tommy into the bathroom where they stayed for a long time with the shower running. It was hot and steamy.

147

For the rest of the morning Tommy had to stay on the sofa. Every five minutes Didi felt his forehead and wiped his nose. Then she opened up a big purple jar.

"Just a bit of this spread on your front will help you breathe better," she said. She rubbed the awful-smelling paste on Tommy.

SMELLY RUB

"Hey look, Tommy!" said Stu, coming in from the kitchen. "Your Grandma Minka brought over some old-country chicken soup. Still has the chicken feet in it!"

Later that day Tommy's friends came over. Didi made sure Tommy was placed on the couch, far away from his friends. "Look what I have, Tommy!" said Didi, coming into the room with a big green suction cup.

"This will help unstuff your nose," she assured him.
"Waaaaaaah!" cried Tommy's horrified friends.
Tommy could only whimper.

"I don't thing I can take this anymore!" snuffled Tommy
miserably. "I godda find that bug and led id go!"

"What bug, Tommy?" asked Chuckie.

"The bug I caught ad the playgrowd! It must have got into
the diaper bag, but when I looked id was gone. It's gotta be in
the house somewhere!" said Tommy.

"We'll help you look for it," said Phil.

"Yeah, we'll find it," said Lil.

The babies searched everywhere.

"Is it big, Tommy?" asked Chuckie.

"Prob'ly," said Tommy.

"Should we smoosh it if we find it?" asked Lil.

"No!" said Tommy. "We gotta uncatch it! I mean, we gotta let it go!"

"Now, here's your medicine," said Didi as she returned with a cup. "I mixed in twenty-seven drops of distilled holistic oil of wheat grass into your juice. You won't even taste the medicine."

Luckily for Tommy, the phone rang. "That must be Dr. Lipschitz calling from his European lecture tour!" she said, jumping up.

While she was gone, Tommy slipped the cup of medicine to Chuckie, who hid it behind a plant.

The next day Tommy felt a tiny bit better.

"I don't know," said Didi. "He's still stuffed up. Maybe I should call Lipschitz again."

"Nonsense!" said Grandpa Lou. "In my day we didn't have fancy doctors—just took lots of doses of cod-liver oil. That did the trick."

"Great idea!" said Didi, running for the medicine cabinet.

"Keep looking for that bug!" Tommy said to his friends when they came over to visit. "I don't thing I can take any more of thad odd-liver oil."

"Cheer up, Tommy," said Chuckie. "Maybe the bug will fly away by itself."

"Hey, maybe we should open up all the windows and doors," said Phil.

"Maybe we should call the exgerminator," suggested Lil.

Suddenly Tommy's dog Spike growled. He stood stock-still as he stared at something in the corner.

"What is id, ol' boy?" Tommy whispered.

Baying loudly, Spike rushed to the corner and stopped, staring. Tommy and his friends followed. There, behind the plant, was Tommy's abandoned cup of medicine from the day before. And crawling on top of it was a tiny . . . bug.

"I don't like this one bit," said Chuckie fearfully. "That bug could be dangerous."

"Maybe we should call a growed-up," said Lil.

"Nah," said Tommy. "I caught id once, I can catch id again!"

Tommy gently trapped the bug inside his bottle.
Chuckie opened the door. Carefully, gently, Tommy
set the bug free.

"Do you feel any better now?" asked Chuckie.

"Maybe a little," said Tommy.

The next morning Didi went to check up on Tommy.

"Why, Tommy, you look so much better!" she exclaimed. "And here I was coming to bring you a get-well present! It's a mobile with exotic insects from the rain forest." After fastening the mobile to his crib, Didi went to tell Stu the good news.

"Here, boy!" Tommy whispered to Spike, as he removed the mobile. "No more bugs for this baby. But I bet this'll make the perfect chew toy."

Spike stood on his hind legs and barked happily.

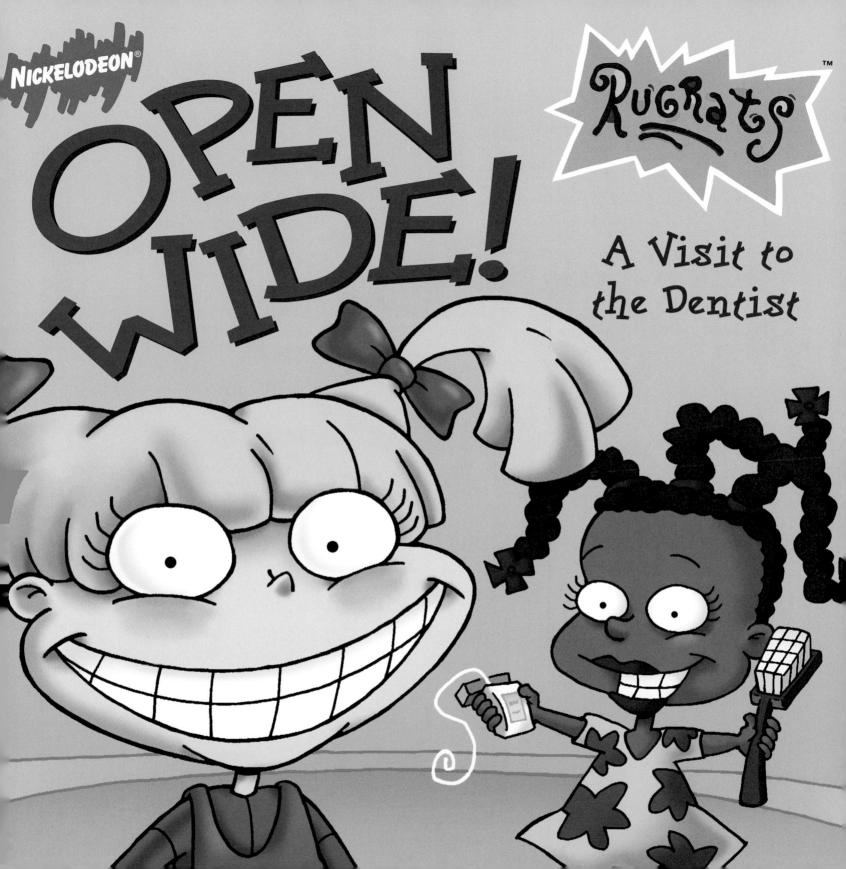

OPEN WIDE!

A Visit to the Dentist

by Cecile Schoberle

illustrated by Barry Goldberg

"Hey, you babies! Guess who I get to go see?" said Angelica.

"Who, Angelica?" asked Chuckie.

The babies were playing in Tommy's front yard. Angelica's dad, Drew, had brought her over to visit.

"I get to go see the dentist," said Angelica. "Just like a growed-up does. You babies are too young to go."

"Why do you get to go see Dennis?" asked Lil.

"Who's Dennis?" asked Phil.

"My daddy said the dentist looks at your teeth," said Angelica.

"We're both going," said Susie. "'Because we've got all of our teeth already."

"Yeah, but you babies don't," said Angelica. She flashed a big, mean smile.

"So why does Dennis look at toofies?" asked Tommy.

"To count 'em," said Angelica.

Tommy tried to get a closer look inside Angelica's mouth. "How many do you have?" he asked.

"Um, about a hunnert billion," Angelica said.

"Hey, I gotta idea!" exclaimed Tommy. "Let's count everybody's toofies."

"Yeah!" shouted Phil. "Me first!"

"No, me first, Philip!" yelled Lil.

Tommy looked in Chuckie's mouth. "One . . . two . . . tree . . . eighty . . . hmm, what number comes next?" he said.

"This is so dumb!" sighed Angelica.

"Teeth help you eat your lunch," said Susie. She crunched on an apple.

"It looks like Chuckie ate spinach," said Tommy.

Tommy's dog, Spike, trotted by as he carried a bone.

"Gee, Spike's toofies look sharp," said Phil.

"I'll bet Reptar's are super sharp!" said Tommy.

170

"Do you guys remember that TV show about beavers?" asked Lil.

"Yeah, beavers got big toofies. They chewed up a whole tree," said Phil.

"How come?" asked Chuckie.

"Uh, I think they like to make toofpicks," said Phil.

"You know what? Some toofies swim," said Tommy.

"What do you mean?" asked Angelica.

"I saw Grampa's toofies swimming in a glass jar all by themselves," said Tommy.

"Well, my daddy told me I'm going to get a present from the dentist," said Angelica. "A *special* toothbrush!"

"A magic one?" asked Phil.

"Or one that talks like that dolly we saw in the store?" asked Lil.

"Maybe it's got jingle bells," said Tommy.

"You dumb babies! I'm going to get a Cynthia toothbrush like I saw on TV, with shiny gold stars all over it!" said Angelica.

Drew came over to Angelica. "We're taking Susie with us to the dentist's office, Angelica. Her daddy will meet us there," he said.

"We'll stop by, too," said Didi. "After you're finished, we'll all go out to lunch at Burger Doodle."

Drew took Angelica and Susie by the hand. "It's time to show Dr. Pearlies what beautiful teeth you have, my dears."

"Hey, didn't Li'l Reddy Hood say something like that in the story my daddy read us?" whispered Chuckie to Tommy.

"Yeah, I hope they don't meet any woofs on the way," said Tommy.

Angelica and Susie arrived at the dentist's office.

"Do we get cookies?" Angelica asked the lady at the desk.

"Oh, no," she said. "You shouldn't eat too many cookies. They're bad for your teeth."

174

Angelica said to Susie, "Do you think the dentist can tell how many chocolate chip cookies I ate?"

Susie said, "You mean like Santa knows when you've been bad?"

Angelica said, "Yeah, maybe the Tooth Fairy knows too, and she told the dentist!"

The dentist's helper took Susie into one room, while Drew took Angelica into a room across the hall. Susie waved as Angelica's daddy helped her climb into a big chair.

"Hello, Angelica! I'm Dr. Pearlies!" said the dentist. "We're going to have fun today. First I'm going to take a picture of your teeth."

Angelica loved to have her picture taken. "Make sure you get my best side," she said.

"Mr. Pickles, let's go look at the x-rays," said Dr. Pearlies. They stepped into the hall.

Susie called out to Angelica from the other room, "Hey, Angelica! Do you have a squirty water-hose thing in your room too?"

"Yes, and lots of shiny things," replied Angelica. "Hey, look, Cynthia!" she said to her doll. "Are you ready for the dentist?"

Angelica looked at all of Dr. Pearlies' shiny things.
"Cynthia, I wonder what that brushy thing does?"
asked Angelica as she pointed. "Oh, Cynthia, are you
scared? But Dr. Pearlies seems so nice. Wait, Cynthia!
Don't run away!"

The doll flew across the room.

Angelica called, "Oh, no! I'm coming, Cynthia!"

Angelica was upset. "Oh, my poor Cynthia!" she yelled. Angelica grabbed a cup and flipped a little switch that turned on the water faucet. Water gushed to the floor. She raced over to Cynthia and tried to give her a drink.

Drew and Dr. Pearlies came back into the room. Drew held up the x-ray pictures. He said, "Just as I thought. My little princess has perfect . . . AARRGH!"

The place was a mess!

"Princess, what happened?" asked Drew.

Angelica held up her doll. "Look, Daddy! Cynthia's got no cavitrees!"

Out in the waiting room, Didi arrived with the babies
to pick up the girls.

"What a cute baby!" the receptionist exclaimed. Dil gurgled.

"What do you think Angelica and Susie are doing right now?"
Chuckie asked Tommy.

"Maybe they get to try out wearing new kinds of toofies," said
Tommy.

"Yeah, like a beaver!" said Phil.

"Or like Spike!" said Lil.

184 "Or like Reptar!" said Tommy.

Angelica and Susie went back to the waiting room.
Susie's dad, Randy Carmichael, had just arrived.

"Hello, Susie!" said Randy.

"Hi, Daddy!" Susie exclaimed. "Look at these great
party bags we got!"

"What's inside, dear?" asked Randy.

"Are there any chocolate chip cookies?" asked Angelica.

"No, but there's lots of other cool stuff," said Susie.

"Just gimme my toothbrush with the gold stars!" said Angelica
as she dug through her bag.

"Did you get a Cynthia toothbrush with gold stars on it, Angelica?" asked Tommy.

Angelica couldn't find one. "No, but I got something *much* better!" she said. "I got a great *big* gold star! All for me! 'Cause I did so good at the dentist!"

"Wow!" said Tommy. "I can't wait till I have lots of toofies. Then I can get a big gold star too!"

ANGELICA

CONGRATULATIONS
ON YOUR FIRST
VISIT TO THE DENTIST

188

Look for these and other Rugrats books—including chapter books and novels for older readers—at your favorite store!

And don't miss the Rugrats in Paris movie books!

SHAPED PAPERBACKS

Ice Cream Fun Day
Once Upon a Reptar
Angelica's Awesome
    Adventure with Cynthia!
Be Brave, Chuckie!
Lights, Camera, Dil!
Bowling Twins

SHAPED BOARD BOOKS

It's a Circus!
Tommy and Chuckie on the Go!
The House that Chuckie Built
Sweet Victory

10X8 PAPERBACKS

The Rugrats' Book
    of Chanukah
Let My Babies Go!
The Bestest Mom
Vacation!
The Turkey Who Came
    to Dinner
The Rugrats Movie Storybook
Runaway Reptar!
Tricked for Treats!
Be My Valentine!
Discovering America
No Place Like Home